COFFEE, MILK

&

Spider Silk

COYOTE JM EDWARDS

Here's to everyone who took a chance on something new.

Here's to ~~~~ who took a chance on ~~~~
something else.

"Listen, listen, listen," Jax said, as Gwen peeked through the lounge door. She caught a glimpse of something colorful on a shelf before he shuffled in front of it, his bare hooves loud on the hardwood floor. Gwen had known this satyr for thirty years—what he thought looked subtle was a neon sign to her. "I get you said you didn't want a farewell party, but . . . well, we couldn't send you off with no ceremony or nothing at all, right?"

All of Gwen's coworkers were assembled in the lounge of the Guardhouse. Here, people came together for a quick lunch, or a quick rant about the traffic, or a quick game of cards while waiting for a citizen to call. The sofas were old and worn; she'd napped on them between shifts a hundred times, despite complaints that her legs took up too much space. In the center of the coffee table, surrounded by old cup rings, sat a framed photo of the newest trainees and their mentors. Gwen had been so proud of them when the picture was taken, visibly crying behind the row of red uniforms.

Contrary to what most believed, it wasn't the job of being a Guard that Gwen loved so much, but the people she worked with every day—and all of them were here, waiting, ready to say goodbye.

Everyone wore their uniforms, even though most of them were off-duty at this time of night. Gwen hadn't changed out of hers yet, having just finished a quiet shift. Jax, her partner—former partner, as a matter of fact—wiped his eyes on a soggy handkerchief. Though scruffy in appearance, with overgrown brown hair, two horns and the biggest goat ears she'd ever seen, he'd clearly made an effort. His handkerchief was the nice maroon one, not the beige one he'd had since highschool.

Captain Marin, Head of the Guard, straightened as Gwen approached. She'd trained with him, years ago. Everyone thought that Gwen would get the promotion when old Aellyris retired, but she and Marin secretly agreed he would do better with the leadership and Gwen would do better with the teamwork. His posture was pristine, his tusks chipped but professionally shined, and his gruff expression was enhanced by the vicious scar cutting across his face—a reminder of the danger Guards could face. And . . . he was holding a red balloon.

Gwen ducked to get through the doorway. Most of the doors in the guardhouse were big enough to accommodate larger species, but Gwen was a drider. Her eight legs made her several feet taller than Marin, and he wasn't exactly short. Her first shift here, she'd knocked herself out on the doorframe . . . ah, so many memories. "This looks like a party," she said with a suspicious laugh.

"No, it's not," Jax protested, stuffing his handkerchief into his shirt pocket. "It's just a friendly goodbye, that's all."

"There's a balloon," Gwen said. She pointed at it.

Captain Marin cleared his throat. "It's . . . it's just . . ." He gazed around at the assorted guards, many of which Gwen had either trained with or helped to train once she decided to leave. When nobody chimed in to save him, he cleared his throat loudly. "It's just a . . ."

The centaur behind him, Leis, spoke up with a bright smile. "It's tradition!" they chirped.

"Right, right," Jax said, nodding quickly. He gave Leis an approving clap of his hands. "Tradition. Right. Not a—"

"What's that hidden behind your back, Jax?" Gwen inquired, already bringing her hands up to her face in excitement.

"Tradition," Jax said immediately.

"Tradition?" Gwen said.

"Right you are. There's *tradition* behind me, that's all and don't you think nothing of it." He nodded again and crossed his arms, as though daring her to make a fuss.

Gwen laughed. "Oh?" she said, peering over his shoulder.

"Just give her the damn thing," Marin said, rubbing his temples.

Jax sighed dramatically and shuffled out of the way. On the shelf sat a lumpy cake with neon blue frosting. In squiggly letters, she could just barely make out the words, *Goodbye Gwen, our bEst Guard,* and something that might have been a flower, or a beach ball. He'd made the cake himself, then. Baking and Jax didn't mix, but he'd clearly given it a good effort.

"There's a balloon and a cake," Gwen said, grinning. "All the evidence points to this being—Captain? You're not crying, are you?"

Marin waved a frustrated hand at her. "Just let us tell you goodbye, alright?" he said, covering his face. He accepted a handkerchief from Jax, mopping his tears as though scrubbing his green skin off. "Damn it to hell—I just can't believe you're leaving us."

"You're one of the best guards I've ever worked with, Gwen," Leis said, crossing their arms.

Roberta put a hand to her heart, her big moth eyes peering up at Gwen with determination. "I'll make you proud," she said, puffing her fuzzy chest up. "I'll—I'll do everything like you taught me—and I won't forget to lock the back door again, I swear."

Gwen put one set of hands on her hips and shook her head. "I'm only going a few blocks down!" she said, laughing. "The way you're all talking, it's like I'm moving to another country or something. You can come visit me, just as soon as the cafe's open." She smiled around at them, seeing them relax at her casual tone.

Marin reached upward, trying to put a hand on her shoulder. He couldn't quite make it, so he settled on the elbow of her middle arm. "Gwen Khetosni," he said, looking up at her. Through the tears, through the gruffness, she saw his bottom lip quiver. "We're sad to see you go. But the truth of the matter is that we're all so proud of you for taking this next step."

Gwen wrung her upper set of hands together, the others letting go of her hips. It was all so much. Marin was their rock—how could she possibly stay composed? Tears rose to her eyes. "Captain . . ."

"Whatever happens," Marin said, looking her in the eye, "we believe in you, and we believe in your cafe."

The others murmured softly in agreement. Someone sniffled.

Marin dabbed his eyes again, cleared his throat and let go of Gwen's arm. "Alright, people," he said, as though commanding an army. "Sappy time is over. Let's cut that cake, I think Jax is trying to steal a bite while we're all sobbin' over Gwen."

"What? No, never!" Jax yelped, snatching his hands back.

The room descended into comfortable conversation, laughter, and teasing—the way the lounge was supposed to be. Jax passed out slices of cake on paper plates, while Roberta fought to open a bottle of champagne. Some of them had been around for what felt like forever, while some had only finished training last month—but they were closer than family, every one of them. The teasing was gentle, the laughter shared rather than at anyone's expense. The warm atmosphere felt like home.

She would miss it, for sure. She knew everyone by name, knew what they were good at, had helped people and saved lives side by side with them. No matter where she went, she'd cherish these connections forever.

But deep in her heart, she knew she was ready to move on. Thirty years of guarding the streets of Embervein was a long time, after all. Today, she would begin to *feed* the streets of—she would *hydrate* the streets—give coffee to the streets of . . .

Well, she could work on the mission statement later.

Embervein didn't have many humans in it. It'd been shielded from the outside by old, powerful magic. Elsewhere in the world, monsterfolk had to disguise themselves, try to mingle among humans or hide in the shadows—but Embervein was a gleaming bubble of safety, a place where they could comfortably express their culture. Even at night, the city bustled with life and love. Nocturnal families got breakfast together, moths and vampires went to work for the day, students hunted for the best venues to study or relax. And Gwen's new cafe would be in the center of it all.

"It's an easy walk from the bus stop," Gwen said to Jax as they trotted along the busy street. Her breath hung in the air as she spoke, illuminated by the street lights and the glowing tiles of the sidewalk. Jax had listened to her rambles about the cafe for months now, but hadn't seen the actual location; she could barely hold still. "Picture it like this: You get off the bus stop, you're on your way to work . . ." She made a rolling motion with her hand to indicate that Jax should continue the idea.

"Ooh, right, so I'm walking down Main Street on my way to work," he said, immediately understanding what she meant. "And I pass by your little cafe . . ."

"With the outdoor seating," Gwen added quickly, "once I find some tables and chairs." The college students from Vi'troth would probably *love* to sit outside.

Jax laughed. "With outdoor seating, right," he said, rubbing his hands together conspiratorially—or to warm them up. "And I see it's a cafe. And I think to myself, boy! Am I hungry!" They went around a cluster of harpies examining a map. Someone gave them a polite nod; even out of uniform, they recognized Jax and Gwen from their hundreds of shifts around the city.

"And maybe you're tired because it's early in the morning," Gwen said, a grin spreading across her face.

"And I'm just *so tired* that I could really use some caffeine," Jax said. "And I see that the little cafe, which serves multiple kinds of breakfast foods, as well as all kinds of coffee—"

"Some of it with latte art," Gwen said.

"—and I think, what luck!" He threw his hands up as though stumbling upon something profound and skipped sideways. Gwen laughed. "What a lucky man am I, that this cafe is right here—why don't I stop in and get something on my way to work?"

"You've got it, that's it exactly!" Gwen said, cupping her face in her upper hands as she laughed. "Doesn't that sound so wonderful?"

"It sounds pretty damn wonderful," Jax agreed. "Where's it at, then? This cafe of wonder?"

Gwen dashed forward, moving quicker than him on her eight legs. He had to sprint to keep up. This section of Main Street was a little quieter, the sidewalk clearer, so she didn't worry about running anyone over. They stopped in front of the cafe—or the building that would become the cafe. *Her* building.

The front window was cracked and dusty, and the paint on the door was peeling like an old sunburn, but she could see the magic, the potential it all held. Soon, she'd replace the trim, paint it all a nice blue or brown, and hang up a great big sign so that everyone would know the cafe's name—which was to-be-determined, but it'd be a *good* name. Right now, nobody looked twice at this sad, crumbling building, but it wouldn't stay that way for long.

She undid her shawl pin with one set of hands, clasped the middle ones in excitement and unlocked the door with the lowest. It stuck for a moment; she shoved with her shoulder until it crunched open.

"Prepare to be amazed," she said, grinning back at Jax as she ducked through the door. It wasn't sized to fit her yet; that would change soon enough.

"I'm prepared," Jax said, pressing his hands together.

Gwen flipped the light on.

A big, empty room greeted them, lit by a single lightbulb. Much of the ceiling plaster had fallen, revealing bare insulation and beams. The floor was no better; much of the wood showed water damage, and the boards in the corner were splintered and broken. A lone coat rack stood in the middle of the mess, surrounded by damp, empty cardboard boxes. On the wall, an

---

open doorway revealed what was once a bathroom: white tile, brown grit, a toilet missing its seat, and a sink on the ground. Other doors led to places she didn't particularly want to think about right now, given that they looked even worse.

The light bulb flickered, threatening to go out as Gwen shut the door.

She wrung all of her hands together. "It's not much," she said. The realtor had hesitated to sell it to her, suggesting that she purchase a smaller place a few streets away—but this one had everything she needed, didn't it? A big room and space outside for tables, something that could become a kitchen with hard work. There was even a side door around the back which led to another empty room. She could host classes there, once it had a floor, a ceiling, and some walls without holes in them.

But considering she had never renovated a building in her life, maybe this was . . . a little ambitious.

"Hey! You've got your own coat rack!" Jax said, grinning as he hung his coat and scarf on it. His ears flopped with excitement. "Sure, it's not much right *now,* but all it needs is a little TLC." He glanced over. "What's with the long face?"

"I don't know," Gwen said, letting her shoulders drop. She scuffed a couple feet against a lumpy floorboard. Pieces broke off. "What if I'm not cut out for this? I've been in the Guard since I was a teenager. Maybe I can't do something else. Maybe I don't know how."

Jax's ears pressed back. He never did like a serious conversation. "But I reckon you can figure it out," he said.

"What if I'm too old to figure it out?"

"Oh, no, you don't," Jax said, wagging a finger in her face. He examined some of the floorboards as well, kicking away a chunk of drywall to reveal some centipedes, who scattered in the sudden light. "Don't you go all midlife-crisis on me, miss. You're not even sixty! When you hit a hundred or so, *then* you can talk about being too old for stuff."

Gwen followed him as he wandered over to the bathroom, picking her way through the mess. "You're not wrong," she said. "But I still don't know if this is right for me. I can't even pick a name for this old place. It has to be the best name. The *right* name. This building contains all my hopes for the future," she said, patting the wall affectionately. "It needs—"

The drywall beneath her hand crumbled and burst across the floor, sending up a cloud of dust.

Jax burst out laughing. "This place is falling apart," he said, coughing as he stumbled out of the cloud. He grinned at her, his woodland-brown hair, scruffy beard, and curling horns now brushed with white. "It's falling to pieces as literally as possible—and you're worried about a *name?*"

It took weeks of hard work, but slowly, the cafe began to look less like a home for stray cockroaches and more like . . . well, a cafe. Somewhere to be! The floors were torn out and replaced with a warm, shiny darkwood. The walls were given fresh drywall, though still needed paint. The door was resized—mostly made wider, for wheelchairs and eight-legged friends. And the huge storefront window was replaced, all shiny and crystal clear, easy to see through from either side.

Gwen was oddly proud of the bathroom, though. She ripped the cracked tiles out herself and replaced them with drywall and wood flooring, and then she painted the walls a soothing blue. The fixtures all matched, and not just that, but the sink and toilet were actually connected to the waterline, meaning they functioned as well as looked nice. There was even a soap dispenser and a paper towel dispenser. As she finished hanging up the brand-new mirror, Gwen took a moment to catch her breath.

She'd never been particularly pretty, or particularly ugly, not even for her own kind. On the whole, she felt quite neutral about her appearance, and that was the general opinion of others, as well. It had never affected her work with the Guard, so it had never mattered.

Her skin was dark like a midnight sky, lighter around her palms, with a scattering of silver freckles on her face and arms—that was normal enough for a drider these days, since everyone spent so much time above ground. Her eight legs were black and fuzzy, and they made her twice the height of nearly everyone she met, but they weren't anything special. She had a blocky face, a wide nose, eight thin, dark eyes, and a mouth like she was perpetually sucking a lemon. Her bluish hair, streaked with grey, was pulled back in a low bun.

She hadn't paid much attention to her appearance since she was a teenager, but right now, she rather thought she looked like a store owner. Or a Store Owner, with capitalization. It was probably the apron, she decided; she'd worn this cozy sweater plenty of times, and it never made her look professional. Or perhaps . . . was it because she owned a store now?

"You picked the most complicated damn tables on Earth," Jax called, and she heard a clattering of wood. Boxes were stacked left and right. Jax sat in the middle of the floor with a screwdriver, a pile of wooden pieces and some instructions in his hand.

"You'll figure it out," Gwen said with a gentle laughter. "You always say it's impossible to start with."

Jax held up a leg and compared it to the larger structure. "Lucky I like you," he said. "I had a thought this morning that I'd steal all your tables and sell them for computer parts. Building *computers* is easier than this."

"You don't know how to build computers," Gwen said.

He let the whole thing clatter to the ground, fixing her with a grumpy stare. "I'll sell 'em for donuts, then," he said. "I know how to eat a damn donut."

Motion through the front window caught Gwen's eye. When she looked over, she found a fluffy brown minotaur peeking in. She wore a blazer with a flower in her pocket and clutched a manila folder in both hands. The minotaur caught Gwen's eye and smiled brightly, coming inside before Gwen could think to stop her. "Hello there!" she sang. "I heard someone was finally fixing this old place and I ran right over here to say hello." She paused, not sure whether to approach Jax or Gwen.

"Don't look at me," Jax said. "I don't run this place. *She* does." He pointed at Gwen. "I'm just the poor innocent soul who got roped into helping out for no money."

"Oh, you stop it," Gwen said, walking overtop of him as he ducked. As tall as she was, his hair didn't even brush her underbelly, but he was annoyed nonetheless. She held a hand out to the woman as she straightened her apron and patted her hair. "I'm Gwen. It's a pleasure to meet you, ah . . . ?"

"Olympia," the minotaur said, smiling brightly as they shook. She had a build like an eighteen-wheeler, and her thick hand nearly enveloped Gwen's long fingers entirely, but her handshake was dainty. "It's going to be a cafe, isn't it? That's what I heard. It's beautiful already!"

"Yes," Gwen said, perhaps with more pride than was justified. It was just a big room with some unbuilt tables, after all. "I'm going to serve coffee and pastries."

"Oh, I *love* coffee," Olympia said. She brushed Gwen's apron. "You had some fuzz. I do love coffee, you know, I have two toddlers—I live off the stuff! You'll be hiring someone to help you work the counter, won't you?"

Such energy! Gwen found herself smiling. "Of course," she said. "I'm looking to hire two baristas, at least to start off. Why do you ask?"

Olympia held the manila folder out to her. "That has my resume and my CV all laid out," she said, beaming like a soft, mud-brown lighthouse. "I would love to help your cafe get going! Oh, by the way,

I couldn't find it anywhere—what's the cafe called?"

Gwen winced, glancing at Jax. "It's called—"

"Don't you dare say 'Afternoon Delight,' that's a sex thing, I said absolutely not," Jax said, pointing threateningly with a table leg.

"Well . . ."

"*Or* 'What Do You Bean By That,'" Jax said. "It's too long. Even if it's funny." He snickered to himself as he put a screw in.

Gwen sighed, thumbing through the pages of the folder. Each document was neatly formatted and smelled lightly of perfume, like Olympia. "It's under development," she said. "I'm . . . working on it." She'd been *working on it* for months now, since the first time she thought about starting a cafe.

Olympia ran a hand through the fluffy fur on top of her head, idly shaping it around her two thick horns. "What about Gwen's Cafe?" she suggested. "Short and simple. It's *your* cafe, after all."

Oh, what a perfect name! Wait—after all this time, it was that simple?

"She's not wrong," Jax said, shrugging. He tried it out: "Gwen's Cafe ... Seems good enough to me. You don't need any of that fancy stuff—get right to the point!"

Gwen laughed, her hands coming to rest on her chest and cheeks. "I ... I like it! it's just what this place needs," she said, feeling a grin spread across her face. "You've solved it, Olympia."

"You can finally order that sign for the front," Jax said.

Olympia lifted her chin with a satisfied smile. "I'm just happy I could help out," she said. "Take a look at my resume, won't you? I'd really love to work with you."

"I will," Gwen said, looking at the file in her hands. Outgoing, headstrong, a mother, and creative. "You'd have to fill out an application, of course, once we have one."

Olympia beamed. "I'd be happy to," she said.

"And then there would be interviews— and there's no guarantee that you'd get the position," Gwen added. "If several people apply, then we'll choose the best person for the job, and that might not be you."

"I understand entirely."

"And," Gwen said, in the interest of being completely honest, "it's not necessarily an *easy* position, either. Since we're a small business, you'll—that is, *if* you got the position, you would have a lot of responsibilities."

"I understand, and I believe that I'm up for the challenge," Olympia said with a laugh, heading toward the front door. "Thank you for considering me! I hope I'll see you again soon."

"Yes," Gwen said. "Have a good day!" she added, because it felt like the thing to do. This apron was giving her all sorts of ideas. She turned and found Jax smirking as he hammered a nail in place. "Oh? What's that look for?"

He chuckled. "You going on about applications and interviews," he said, shaking his head. "You love her! She's already got the job."

"Well, I have to act professional," Gwen said, smiling as she brushed her hands over her apron. "Can't go around hiring people on a whim and all that. But you know what, I bet you're right—I think she's our first barista."

"Our?" Jax said, glancing up. He poked at her with his hammer. "You mean *your*. It's your name on the building—at least, once you get that sign."

Imagine that! A set of tables, a fun barista, and a sign with her name on it. Sometimes her dreams seemed so much closer than they looked.

The cafe now had a beautiful front counter and a glass display case to show off all the pastries they'd be offering. Jax installed a giant chalkboard menu. Gwen had imagined something less messy, but it'd been a good price, and she had neat handwriting anyway. They'd figured out the tables and most of the chairs, and painted the walls light-brown—like a latte—with one dark accent wall in the back. The sign out front said *Gwen's Cafe* in looping letters. And the kitchen, best of all, had everything she and Olympia would need: spacious silver countertops, coffee grinders, a big oven, two espresso machines and a huge refrigerator for all the ingredients.

Of course, Olympia had gotten the job. Less than a week after dropping off her resume, Olympia had memorized every single latte recipe *and* organized the kitchen for maximum efficiency. How wonderful was that?

Everything was nearly perfect, nearly ready for her to open the cafe, but she still lacked some crucial pieces. Such as cups, outdoor furniture, and a second barista. Right now, she and Jax were waiting on . . . well, all of those things. They had two deliveries coming, and hopefully, someone would want a job soon. Gwen stood behind the counter and tried to create latte art.

"You're really determined to make your lattes fancy," Jax said from his stool on the other side. He watched her carefully bring a pitcher of steamed milk to a mug on the counter. "I never saw the point. You make it look like a puppy or something, and then people drink it. What's cute about eating puppies?"

"If it's pretty, they'll take pictures and post them to the internet," Gwen said, taking a deep breath. She tucked a lock of greying hair behind her ear and began to slowly pour the milk into her coffee, like she'd seen in an online video. "It's free advertising. Not to mention, it just looks nice, I think. I can't do puppies as of right now, though."

She moved the pitcher around as she poured, like she'd seen in the video, but the milk just vanished beneath the surface of the coffee. Slowly, the whole thing turned a creamy brown, with no visible shape or design. Gwen sighed. A good cup of coffee, maybe, but not art.

"I think your milk's too thin," Jax said, peering into the cup.

"You might be right," Gwen said. She slid the mug toward him. "Here you go. On the house, for all your hard work."

His soft goat ears perked up. "Thanks!"

Gwen knelt down so she could lean with her elbows on the counter, looking out at the busy afternoon street. Monsterfolk passed by on the sidewalks, talking on their phones or with each other, rushing from one place to the next without even glancing at the cafe.

"So many people," Gwen said. "You'd think one of 'em would want to work in a nice place like this."

"Yeah, well, most people wouldn't know a good opportunity if it slapped them on the ass."

An older neko woman, her cat ears greying like the rest of her hair, paused to look at their hiring sign. She had a baby stroller with her; the child had a rubber toy designed to look like a ball of yarn in her hands and she chewed on it with glee, her pointed tabby tail twitching playfully. The woman looked too old to be her mother but they seemed to share the same nose and eyebrows ... her grandmother, perhaps. Maybe they were out for a walk, spending some quality time together while Mom rested at home.

How nice that must be: enjoying the fresh air with a babbling baby. Gwen sighed, watching the kitten drop her toy; the woman picked it up and handed her a fresh one before they continued down the street.

Jax followed her gaze. "Oh, no," he said. "You're not getting baby fever, are you? Gods above, my sister was baby crazy for *months*, drove me batty. She couldn't look at a kid in an advertisement without bursting into tears. I cheered like a banshee when she announced the pregnancy—everyone thought I was nuts, but they didn't have to live with her!"

"I'm not getting baby fever," Gwen said, laughing. "Well—I don't know. I don't want to be a mother, that sounds like too much work. Don't care to get married. But I love children. Can't I just skip to being a grandma?"

"I don't think that's how that works," Jax said, stirring more sugar into his coffee. "Pretty sure, you know, genetics and all . . ."

Gwen shrugged. "Being a grandma is the fun part," she said. "You get to hug the kids and give them presents, and they love you no matter what, because you don't ever have to tell them off."

"You got that right, and being an uncle is great, too, minus the baby fever stuff," Jax said, as though he knew all about it. He brightened. "Hey, you know what? You want to be a grandma? How do you feel about teenagers?"

Gwen considered it. She'd been a teenager once, a long time ago—though drider adolescence continued well past the teen years. "Can't say I've spent much time around them," she said.

"But they're fine. Why? What're you scheming?"

Jax rubbed his hands together. "I think I found you your next barista," he said. "And a grandkid! You remember my cousin Lackadaisy?"

"The one who got caught in that magical explosion?" Gwen said, racking her brain. Jax's extended family made up less of a tree and more of a forest. She'd attended one family reunion with him before, and had managed to forget the names of nearly everyone who mattered.

"That's the one! Her kid just turned sixteen and she's all ready for her first job. Wants independence and such." He threw back the last of the coffee and wiped his beard. "You wait here, I'll go see if she's off school yet." With a grin, he added, "You're gonna love her."

Gwen nodded. Jax was a good judge of character, and who better to help run the cafe than family? She watched him trot out to his car. While she waited, she could try some latte art again.

His car returned half an hour later and bore the most miserable teenager Gwen had ever seen. Her hair, made up of vining leaves, was tangled and wilted. Her eyes were the color of moss, made to look smaller and perhaps bruised with black eyeliner. She wore a faded t-shirt and baggy, ripped shorts that showed off two white prosthetic legs. As she stepped onto the curb, she stumbled, grabbing onto Jax's arm to steady herself; when she glanced at him, Gwen saw a hearing aid fitted onto her ear.

Gwen tried to remember where dryads fitted into Jax's family forest and if she was supposed to know this kid's name. "Hello," she called, as they came inside.

Jax grinned widely. "I present to you, the one, the only, Mellowmalt Capresh!"

"Nobody calls me that except my moms," the kid said, looking at her tennis shoes. "I just go by Mellie."

Well, that saved her some trouble. "I'm Gwen," Gwen said, smiling at her. "It's nice to meet you."

"Sorry, what?" Mellie looked up, her gaze going to Gwen's mouth.

"I said I'm Gwen, and it's nice to meet you," Gwen said, raising her voice a little. Behind Mellie, Jax gave her a thumbs-up.

Mellie nodded. "Oh, alright."

Jax looked between them. "So, Mellie here wants to work at your fine establishment," he said. "I spoke to her ma and she has the all-clear."

"I don't have a resume," Mellie said. "Not yet. Mom's at work all the time, and Mama just . . . doesn't want to help me, so . . ."

"That's fine," Gwen said quickly. As if she would turn away Jax's cousin for not having a resume! "You can start work today, how about that?"

Mellie shrugged.

Jax clapped his hands together. "Then it's settled! And that's the delivery truck pulling in now, so I'll go get the furniture, and you two can get acquainted." He patted Mellie on the shoulder and went outside. Mellie watched him go.

"I think we're going to make a great team, Mellie," Gwen said, smiling. "I'm excited to work with you! Have you ever—"

"Okay, look." Mellie turned sharply toward her, apparently seeing that Jax was busy. She put her hands on the countertop. The kid was pretty short for a dryad, but her gaze was intense, anyway. "I don't want to work here, but

Mom said I have to. She's always at work, and Mama has all her doctor's appointments and taking care of my sister, so they just want me to do something after school."

Oh, goodness, Gwen hadn't expected that at *all*.

"So, I'll do the job," Mellie said, "but we're not going to be best friends or anything like Cousin Jax wants. Okay? I just want you to know that so we can get on with it."

Gwen tilted her head. She was no expert on teenagers, but ... Poor kid. "Alright, then," she said, nodding. "We can have a professional relationship. Is that what you want?"

Mellie sat back on her heels, letting go of the counter as she nodded. "That's fine," she said.

The door jingled as Jax came back. He put a box on the counter. "There's your cups," he said with a cheerful smile. "And the others are putting your furniture on the patio. How are you doing together?"

Gwen glanced at Mellie. "We're doing just fine. Right, Mellie?" she added, offering her a smile.

Mellie looked at the ground, scuffing her feet against the new wooden floors. If her shoes left a mark—well, Gwen wouldn't get upset, but she'd be unhappy about it. "Yeah," Mellie said. "Basically best friends already."

"Of course," Gwen said.

"Yeah."

"Right."

Jax beamed at them both. "I just *knew* you two would get along like peaches and cream," he said.

The cafe had everything it needed for its first day: freshly baked danishes drizzled with a cream cheese glaze, two dozen cupcakes with perfect spirals of white frosting, espresso machines hot and ready, bottles of syrup, and whipped cream lined up along the counter. Gwen had carefully handwri tten the current menu and cleaned all of the tables. And Olympia was given the honor of flipping the sign from *CLOSED* to *OPEN*.

The only thing the cafe lacked was anyone to serve.

"It's still early in the day," Olympia said, moving the danishes around in the display case. Gwen had learned quickly that Olympia wanted everything to be neat, tidy, and perfect. To her credit, the danishes looked a lot nicer lined up by size rather than thrown haphazardly, like Gwen had done.

Mellie sighed, putting her head down on the counter. Gwen had found her a comfortable stool, and now she refused to get off it. Some dead leaves spilled from her hair. "This is boring," she groaned.

"If you really want something to do, I'll have you clean the bathroom," Gwen said, watching people pass by on the street.

Mellie shot upright, horrified. "I cleaned it yesterday!" she cried.

"Well, it'd be less boring than sitting here," Gwen said.

Mellie put her head back on her arms and mumbled something unsavory.

"I think," Olympia said, as she took the cupcakes off their stand, "that we shouldn't be disappointed yet. There's still all day—I think, once lunchtime comes around, this place will be packed, and we just won't know what to do!" She grinned at them, and began to thoughtfully set the cupcakes back on the stand.

Gwen adjusted her apron and pinned her name tag to a different spot. Olympia wore her own apron, but Mellie's hung in the kitchen, despite being reminded three times that she needed to wear it. Oh, but what did it matter? They had no customers to see the aprons, the baristas, or the cupcakes Olympia had organized by frosting height.

All this work, and for what? Sitting at the counter, bored out of their minds. They'd worked so hard last night to prepare that they had nothing left to do. They'd prepared for *nothing*. Gwen tried to avoid thoughts like, *You've failed entirely*, and, *What made you think you could do this?* But she didn't have Olympia's unending optimism, so that left her somewhere in the middle: unhappy, uncertain, still somehow hopeful.

Mellie watched some people walk past with her chin resting on her hand. "Did you even advertise this place?" she asked, glancing up at Gwen.

"Once I learn to do latte art, people will take pictures to post online," Gwen said brightly. "Free advertising." She'd heard this wonderful idea from Roberta.

"No, but did you do any advertising yourself?" Mellie asked. She picked some old nail polish off her thumb.

Gwen shook her head. "What do you mean?" she asked.

"Oh," Mellie said, her shoulders slumping. She shoved her hair out of her face. "Yeah, that explains some stuff. You didn't even advertise your own grand opening."

Gwen didn't like her condescending tone. But this was Jax's cousin, or first-cousin-once-removed, or . . . something. She was family, that's what mattered, and Gwen had all the patience in the world for family. "Like an advert on the radio?" she asked.

"No," Mellie groaned. When Gwen still didn't get it, Mellie went on with a sigh. "Who even listens to the radio anymore? I mean *online*. Or in the paper, if you want to get loads of old people in here."

What in the world was she talking about? "I don't understand," Gwen said, looking from Mellie to Olympia.

"Okay, boomer," Mellie muttered.

Olympia straightened. "I think what Mellie's trying to say is that it could help us if you advertised on social media and locally," she said. "The radio isn't a bad idea, but a lot of the younger crowd don't listen to it. Does the cafe have any social media pages?"

Gwen shook her head. She'd never touched social media in her life—though Jax used it to keep up with all of his family members, so she wasn't *completely* oblivious. Her plan was to let the customers use social media for her, like Roberta said.

"That's okay!" Olympia said, reaching out and straightening Gwen's nametag for her. "We can get started on that now, can't we, Mellie? We'll do that for you, Gwen." She winked at Mellie like they had a secret. Mellie looked away.

"Do you know how?" Gwen asked, glancing between them again. Oh, no. Had she shot herself in the foot, not knowing about this?

Olympia nodded, and Gwen felt some of the tension drain from her shoulders. If Olympia knew what to do, then they were saved. "I helped with the PR for a nonprofit a few years ago," Olympia said. "Right after my oldest was born. The first five months, he couldn't sleep if he was away from me, so I'd work from my phone in bed."

Mellie scuffed her shoe against the counter. "It's not like it's hard," she muttered.

"Wonderful," Olympia said, patting her shoulder. "You and I can work on that—and Gwen can make us some of her beautiful latte art," she added. "For practice."

That wasn't such a bad idea. The two ladies huddled together with their phones out, and to Gwen's delight, Mellie actually engaged with Olympia—talking to her, agreeing with her, discussing things that Gwen didn't really understand.

Gwen fetched the milk steamer, a cup, and a small amount of espresso from the machine. If the other two were doing *that* kind of social media, then she would handle the latte art side of things. Roberta's idea was good—and Gwen wasn't completely oblivious; she could do this, and it'd turn out just as well as whatever Mellie and Olympia did.

She steamed the milk until it was frothy and creamy, swirling it around the metal pitcher like she'd seen on the video. It coated the sides, so it wasn't too thin this time. Each failure helped her learn, she reassured herself; this attempt was bound to turn out better than the last. After a deep breath, she slowly poured the frothed milk into the coffee, moving the pitcher from side to side.

The front door jingled. They all looked up in anticipation.

"Hi, um, can I use your restroom?" a small moth-person asked.

Gwen's shoulders slumped. "Of course," she said. "It's just over there." She pointed in the direction of the bathroom and they gratefully went toward it. Gwen resumed the pouring of the milk, hoping the slight interruption wouldn't affect her design. She took her time with it, making sure to hold the pitcher at an appropriate height from the cup. And she didn't pour so fast that it all disappeared under the coffee.

After a few minutes, the moth-person came back out and went straight to the door.

"Would you like anything to drink?" Gwen asked quickly, before they could escape. The tone of her voice was cheerful, casual, even inviting. She employed all of her emotional strength for this task. "On your way? We have a berry mocha you might like." Moth-people were big fans of fruit, she recalled. This wasn't true for *all* of them, but it was a pretty safe bet.

"Tempting, but no, thanks," they said with a laugh. "I'm just passing through."

Her strength gave out and her happy voice vanished. "Have ... have a nice day," Gwen managed, as all six of her arms dropped to her side.

"Oh, Gwen, it's going to be okay," Olympia said, offering her a hug. Gwen accepted, wrapping most of her arms around the minotaur woman, as though they could squeeze the despair away. "It's going to turn out just fine. May I see your latte?" she asked with an unfaltering smile.

Gwen showed it to her.

"That's so nice! Isn't that nice, Mellie?" Olympia said, fixing Mellie with a sharp, motherly stare.

Mellie shrugged. "I guess," she said. "What's it supposed to be?"

"A flower," Gwen said, looking at their faces.

"It looks like poop."

"Mellie!" Olympia cried.

Gwen looked down at her latte. In trying to keep the milk from becoming too thin, like last time, she must have made it too thick. The white foam had entirely covered over the espresso, leaving no distinguishable pattern or detail, aside from some vague lumpiness. She might as well have sprayed whipped cream on top and called it a flower. It wasn't art. It wasn't anything.

Just like the cafe.

Mellie leaned into the kitchen, hanging on the door even though Gwen had asked her not to. It left fingerprints every time. "Gwen," she said. "There's a weird guy with a briefcase and a creepy bird here to see you."

"Oh my goodness!" Gwen immediately slid her tray of half-frosted cupcakes over to Olympia. "Mellie, don't talk like that—those are the boys from the Startup Foundation." Her apron was *covered* in flour. She frantically brushed it away.

"Calm down, it'll be okay," Olympia said, putting the cupcakes aside and helping her.

Mellie let the door close behind her. "What's the Startup Foundation?" she asked.

"Small business startups," Gwen said, fixing her hair out of her face. "They're paying for the cafe to get going, more or less, and we would like them to *keep* doing that until the cafe can pay for itself."

"Oh," Mellie said. "So I shouldn't have asked him why his creepy bird is missing an eye?"

"No! You certainly shouldn't have!"

"It's going to be okay, Gwen," Olympia said. She stepped back. "You look fine! Now go on out there and be confident, you got that?" She smiled.

Gwen didn't return the smile, instead dashing into the cafe. The man standing at the counter wore professional shades of brown, including a patternless tie and some dull loafers. His hair was short, and his expression looked as though he'd recently cut onions. And, as described, a one-eyed owl perched on his shoulder.

"Mr. Manifest," Gwen said. "And Mr. Eve, it's so good to see you both. How can I help you two gentlemen?" Out of the corner of her eye, she saw the kitchen door open *just* a crack, just enough to let people on the other side hear what was happening. She refused to look that way, lest the men see.

Mr. Manifest opened his briefcase and pulled out a manila folder, which he set on the counter between them. "We received the report of your first week," he said, "and we have some concerns."

The owl turned its head sideways and whistled.

"My partner also notes that it is currently lunchtime on a Monday, and your cafe is empty," Mr. Manifest added.

"What are you worried about?" Gwen asked, wringing two of her hands together; the other four wiped crumbs off the pastry case. She could guess why they'd visited. Maybe she was wrong.

"We are concerned that your business may not be sustainable," Mr. Manifest said. Like his partner, his eyes gave off the impression that he was hunting for something small and furry to eat.

"Well, we're just starting out," Gwen said. But she'd had this concern herself, more or less daily since she signed the deed, and she knew her words were empty and uncertain. "Things like this are always slow to start out."

"It is not normal for a cafe to have only ten sales in a week," Mr. Manifest said. "According to our calculations, your cafe has *lost* money every day that it's been open. I hate to say this," he added, with an expression like he couldn't care less, "but if you can't show a profit by the end of the month, we will pull our funding."

Gwen didn't know what to say. Some of her hands wrung themselves, and some of her hands wrung her apron like she wanted to squeeze water out of it.

The owl tilted its head at her and chirped lightly.

"My partner would like to wish you luck, and notes that he has every faith in your ability to turn this business around," Mr. Manifest said, as though he was reciting numbers from a page. Hardly encouraging. "Have a good day, Gwen Khetosni." He turned and walked out of the cafe. The owl's head twisted around and watched Gwen all the way to their car.

The kitchen door burst open. "Oh, Gwen, I'm sure it'll be fine," Olympia said, joining her at the counter. "That man! He was trying to scare you, I'm sure of it. We'll figure this out! We'll show them what we can do!"

"Or we'll crash and burn," Mellie said, hanging on the door. "And all of this will have been for nothing."

Olympia waved her away. "Don't talk like that, Mellie," she chided.

"Why not? I'm just being realistic. Sorry I don't think everything's sunshine and roses, like *you* do."

Gwen put her hands on her hips. "Please don't pick a fight with Olympia," she said. "I—I have plenty enough on my mind without you—"

"Picking a fight?" Mellie straightened, crossing her arms. She'd doodled on them with a marker, black on green. "Is that what you think of me? That I just go around picking fights? That I just *want* to make your life worse? You think *I* don't have problems, too?"

What in the world? Where was this coming from? "Mellie," Gwen said, more sharply than she'd intended. Mellie had been snarky all morning, and Gwen had just about used all her patience already. She couldn't imagine why Mellie would be so antagonistic for no reason. "I think you should take a walk," she said slowly. That would be the best way to deescalate the situation.

"You think your life is sooooo hard because you're too dumb to run a business," Mellie said. She made a *woe is me* face and fell back against the doorway. "At least you have all of your legs! Ever think about that? Eight legs, all of them fine—"

"Mellie, *please*, take a—"

"And you *still* don't know how to work this place! You should have stayed at your old job instead of making me and Olympia *fail* with you."

Oh, that stung. Gwen knew it shouldn't—why did it matter what a dramatic teen thought of her? But it was what she thought of herself, too. This had to stop. Time for the last resort, the trick she'd kept in her pocket since the beginning.

"If you keep this up, I'm going to call your parents," Gwen said.

There, she'd done it—a threat. She'd never actually spoken to Mellie's parents, but the girl seemed like she could keep this tantrum up for a while, and Gwen had to do *something*. It hung in the air between them for several seconds; even Olympia, who had plenty of experience with children, looked between them with widened eyes.

Had she gone too far? Gwen knew Mellie didn't like her parents much, and what could be more of an insult than treating her like a little kid, removing the independence she had here at her job—

Mellie laughed.

Mellie *laughed* and it made Gwen's blood boil.

"Fine!" Mellie spat. "Fine, call my parents! They won't care! They don't *fucking* love me anyway—and you know what, you're right," she added, shrugging so hard Gwen thought her shoulders would hit her ears. "I should take a walk. I'm gonna do that. And I'm *never coming back*."

"That's okay," Gwen said bitterly, even knowing it would only serve to make the girl angrier. "Don't come back, and I'll hire another barista."

"Great! Fine!" Mellie kicked the kitchen door open, leaving a big shoe print, and stormed through. They heard the back door slam.

The kitchen became uncomfortably silent. How was she supposed to feel right now? Frustration burned in her chest, alongside sadness. She looked at Olympia for guidance and found the minotaur grimacing. Oh, heavens above, she'd really messed up, hadn't she, to make positive, optimistic Olympia grimace like that?

"I didn't know what else to do," Gwen said. Her arms hung loosely at her sides. "I—what would you have done? She can't keep treating us like this and not working and—and everything else . . . I've tried talking to her, but she won't listen."

Olympia shook her head. "Don't worry about it," she said. "She'll come back."

Life went on. Mellie returned for her next shift, refusing to talk about what happened, and Gwen didn't call her parents, refusing to give up on her—though secretly, she'd begun to think of the kid as a lost cause, even if she *was* family. And the cafe continued to make very few sales. Half the Guard came in for lunch once, and that was the busiest day they'd ever seen, but it didn't make up for all the empty times before and after.

It was hard for Gwen to stay optimistic about this, though at least she had Olympia, a shining source of determination and positive thinking. When Gwen couldn't imagine their success, she found Olympia and asked her what she envisioned for the cafe's future: usually, something along the lines of crowded tables, long lunch lines, and the need to hire more baristas to keep up with demand. The things that Gwen had hoped for, back when the cafe was a lunch break daydream and not the unfortunate reality in front of her.

A group of college students hesitated in front of the cafe's door, and then decided to go elsewhere. Olympia had stepped out back for a phone call, but maybe if she was finished, she'd be willing to have a chat—at least so that Gwen wasn't forced to watch the people pass. She pattered through the kitchen and pushed open the back door as quietly as possible, in case she was still on the phone.

The minotaur sat in the alley, her phone on the pavement beside her, head in her hands. Oh, no.

"Olympia?" Gwen asked, pushing through the door. "What's the matter, honey?"

Olympia glanced up with her big, round eyes. Her long eyelashes were damp—so she'd been crying, then. "Nothing, nothing," she said, straightening and smoothing her head fur down. "I'll get through it! I'll—I'll figure it out somehow. I'll charge ahead . . ."

Echoes of the words she'd so confidently given to Gwen and Mellie. "But what's the matter?" Gwen said. "What was that phone call?"

"It was my babysitter canceling," Olympia said, looking at her apron and brushing away specks of old leaves. "See? That's not so bad . . . nothing I can't handle." Her voice tightened on the last word and she shut her mouth, as though trying to keep any more weakness from escaping.

Gwen reached down and pulled a ladybug off her horn, gently blowing on her fingers until it flew away. "Then it's not what you're really upset about," she reasoned. "So what's it going to be, hon? You can tell me, or I can keep asking."

"I don't want to be a downer," Olympia said, glancing up at her again. She met Gwen's eyes, and something inside her seemed to give way as her own turned damp and watery. "This was—I'm working here and my side hustle, you know?

Trying to take care of the kids—ever since the divorce—I don't regret it," she said, holding up her hands, "but life was a lot easier when there were *two* of us earning the bread."

Gwen nodded. "You're doing twice as much work," she said. "Do you get child support?"

"Yes, but it isn't . . ." Olympia shook her head. "I won't speak badly of my ex-wife, but let's just say that things are tight."

Gwen nodded again; if Olympia didn't want to talk about it, then she wouldn't force the topic.

"And me and some of the other moms were going out for drinks tonight," Olympia said, busying her hands by straightening her apron and retying it. "But no babysitter. Which is okay, it'll be alright."

"When's the last time you did something that wasn't work or family related?" Gwen asked, though she was pretty sure she knew the answer. Somewhere in the realm of months, at best.

Olympia thought about it as she slowly stood up. "Not since the divorce," she admitted, her ears flicking. "My ex-wife's mom used to watch them sometimes, but not since then. She's mad at me, I think. So is my own mom—but that's not new, she's hated me since I came out as a teen."

"You've got . . . how many little ones? Two, isn't it?" Gwen asked, already putting together a plan. Olympia nodded. "Well, I have six arms! You leave the little ones to me and enjoy your night out." She put some hands on her hips and clasped the rest together.

"Gwen," Olympia said gently, "you're managing the cafe tonight, aren't you? You and Mellie?"

"Me and Mellie will do just fine," Gwen said, laughing. She set a hand on Olympia's arm. "Don't you worry about it! Drop them off here—it's not like it'll be busy." Sad to say, but it was true. She smiled, trying to make up for the sudden void of happiness that Olympia left by being sad. "There, that's all settled, then."

Olympia's ears twitched and she stood on her tiptoes to hug Gwen. Despite the fact that Gwen was so much taller than her, having to lean down to reach comfortably, she felt dwarfed. Olympia leaned back with a big smile on her bovine face. "You're like an angel from the stars, Gwen," she said.

"I'll drop them off just before six, alright? And I'll bring their go-bag and their tablet, and—and, Gwen, you've made my day, you know that, right? And they'll just *love* you."

Well, Jax had said the same thing about Mellie, so Gwen had her doubts. But she'd do her best, of course.

"Wow," Mellie said. "So now I'm a barista *and* a nanny. Great."

Even Mellie's bad mood couldn't get Gwen down. The little ones were absolutely adorable, and Gwen was full of warm, happy feelings. Vasilis, aged five, was currently making a tower of paper cups in his superhero hoodie. On top of his head were little nubs that would grow into horns like his mother's one day. And tiny two-year-old Elias was all giggles and smiles. He toddled over to Mellie.

"Lemon?" he asked, staring up at her.

"You can't just have candy whenever you want," Mellie said, but the force of his eyes was too much to withstand, and she searched their bag for another lemon candy.

He squealed, "Thank you!" and skipped off to see what his brother was doing.

Gwen got out some cleaning spray and began to wipe the counter. "I think he really likes you," she said.

"I guess." Mellie shrugged, leaning against the fridge. "I don't really care."

"Am I remembering correctly that you have a younger sibling?"

"Yeah."

"I bet you're a wonderful big sister," Gwen said, glancing back over her shoulder to smile at her.

Mellie shrugged again, looking at her feet. She was wearing shorts today, and Gwen could see some marker doodles on the white of her prosthetic legs—flowers, pentagrams, little ghosts, and cat faces. "I don't know," she said. "I feel like an *awful* sister. I just spend all my time wishing she was less traumatized so my parents could actually care about me."

That was the most Mellie had said about her feelings in the entire time she'd worked here. Gwen considered her next actions as she made circles on the counter with some damp rags. She had to be careful; she wanted Mellie to feel comfortable talking about things. But before she could say anything else, Mellie went on.

"I know she has problems," she said, crossing her arms, as though self-soothing. "I mean, I lost my legs and some of my hearing, but it didn't really . . . My sister can't sleep at night and stuff, and she freaks out if she smells a hamburger because that's what she was eating when *it* happened. At least I don't have to deal with that."

It. Gwen didn't need to ask; Jax had told her everything at the time. The restaurant was operating a fortunate-octane generator, an unpredictable source of power that ran on luck magic, made illegal because of its tendency to erupt in flame if not used correctly. And frying burgers was *not* using it correctly. Mellie's family had sued the restaurant, but the damage was done. This was the first time Mellie had mentioned it, even in passing.

"But?" Gwen asked. Keeping it simple seemed like a good idea. It left plenty of room for Mellie to fill in whatever she felt like filling in.

Mellie sighed. "But," she said, "I just wish—it hasn't been *easy* for me, you know? My legs hurt all the time and I'm always asking people to repeat themselves . . ."

She shrugged. "But nobody has time for me."

"Go bathroom?" Elias squeaked, tugging on Gwen's shirt.

"Vasilis, can you show your brother where the bathroom is?" Gwen said.

"I'm on it!"

The two raced out of the kitchen, Elias holding onto his big brother's hoodie.

Gwen put the rags down slowly and turned toward Mellie. Focusing on her might scare her away, but she didn't want her to feel ignored, either—especially given what she'd just said. "You can love your sister and wish your parents had more time for you," she said. "You can do both."

"You think so? I don't know." Mellie shook her head. "I—I don't think I'm a good person. I *know* I'm not a good person—I mean, I'm always snapping at you and Olympia even if you didn't do anything wrong, and yesterday I told my sister that my fake leg would come alive and bite her if she didn't get out of my room."

Gwen snorted with amusement and Mellie looked up, utterly betrayed. "Oh no, honey! I wasn't laughing at you," she said quickly. "It just—it's a little bit funny. About your leg coming alive, that is. I don't think that was such a mean thing to do."

The corners of Mellie's mouth twitched. "I thought it was funny, my mom yelled at me for it," she said, covering her mouth, like she didn't want Gwen to see her smile. "She never laughs at anything. One time, I took my leg off and poked her with it and said I was kicking her, and she didn't even smile."

Gwen laughed, and delightfully, Mellie giggled with her. "Mellie, where were you hiding all this humor?" she said, putting some hands on her hips in a mock-stern pose.

Mellie shrugged. "I guess I haven't been happy lately," she said. "Sorry. Um—I'm sorry for being mean to you and Olympia, I just . . . Yeah."

"Honey, it's okay," Gwen said. She reached out and patted her on the arm. "You're family, and sometimes family doesn't get along. That's just fine."

"How am I family?" Mellie said, her eyebrows scrunching together.

"Well, you're related to Jax," Gwen said, "and Jax is part of my family as much as anyone related by blood, so that makes you family whether you like it or not, I'm afraid."

"Oh," Mellie said, with a laugh. "Sure, I guess."

"And that's true even if something happens to the cafe," Gwen said. Such as having to close it. She didn't add that part. "Okay? It's nothing to do with you working here. Family is family."

"I mean, if you say so. Oh, wait . . ." Mellie brightened, almost glowing with sudden excitement. "I meant to tell you! I read some stuff online, and I think I know how to help the cafe." She came over and got a cloth, starting to clean the counter alongside Gwen.

"Oh? How's that?" Gwen said, cleaning again as well.

"We can get more people in here if we have an event," Mellie said. She scrubbed at some dried frosting. Gwen could usually clean faster on her own—six arms, and all that—but Mellie looked surprisingly determined. "Me and Olympia can advertise it online, maybe we could even get the paper to do something about it."

"What kind of an event?" Gwen asked.

"Oh, it could be anything," Mellie said. "The point is that people come in to do something, and then they buy coffee while they're here. I saw some places do a games night, or a coffee-tasting event—though that sounded too posh for us. The coffee tasting, I mean."

It did sound like a reasonable idea—more people inside the cafe, more people buying drinks, and then they'd tell others, and so on . . . "What about something to do with music?" Gwen suggested. "We don't have much of that around here."

"Yeah! Like an open mic night, maybe."

An open-mic night? Gwen pictured people reciting bad poetry and playing the guitar. She remembered the one time they did something like that with the Guard—a public cookout, but then they invited people to do whatever they'd like with a microphone. There'd been a lot of bad singing, but a lot of happy visitors, and that's what mattered. It was perfect. "I like that," she said. "An open mic night! I think that's what the cafe needs, Mellie—I think you've solved it."

Mellie looked down at the countertop, bashful.

"Um," a small voice from the doorway said. Elias hugged his arms, stepping from hoof to hoof. There seemed to be hand soap smeared across his furry face. "Um . . . there's a *mess* . . ."

His brother nearly slammed into him from behind. "Elias did it!" he said, clothes soaked with water. "Elias got soap all over the sink and the floor!"

"No! You did!" Elias squeaked.

Outside of the kitchen, the front door jingled to let them know someone had come into the cafe. A peek through the kitchen door showed a succubus examining the menu with her wallet in her hands.

"Uh, I can clean it up," Mellie said, glancing up at Gwen. She smiled, though it wavered the way someone sways while carrying a heavy object. "So you can serve the customer. I don't mind, it's whatever," she added, before grabbing some towels and going out to the bathroom.

Gwen leaned down to the little ones. "Would you two like to help me take an order?" she asked, and was delighted to see their excitement as they followed her to the counter.

And just like that, there was a little more peace in the cafe.

A week passed. They set a date for the open-mic night, and it loomed like a mountain on the approaching horizon.

Gwen was good with her hands. Well—she was good with her body, in general. And this wasn't some kind of over-blown self-confidence, it was just a fact. She'd worked with the Guard for so long because she could move quickly and deliberately under pressure. She never tripped, stumbled, or knocked into things; she was always aware of what her body was doing and how it related to everything around her. And like any drider, she could use all of her six arms efficiently and simultaneously without getting muddled up or making mistakes. Also, she could knit quite quickly. Call it grace, talent, or skill—Gwen worked well when the task was hands-on.

Except when it came to latte art, apparently.

The countertops were cluttered with used cups, splashes of cream, and sprays of cocoa powder. It smelled like espresso and chocolate; both had spilled on her clothes at least twice. She must have poured twenty, maybe thirty cups of coffee, trying to reuse the drink where she could so as not to waste anything. And they'd all turned out varying levels of *bad*: maybe the design was too mushy, maybe the milk disappeared into the coffee, maybe the coffee was too cold to display a shape properly.

If she couldn't do this next one, she would give up. Forever, not just for tonight.

Did it really matter? No; they weren't even selling latte art yet. But in some small way, this felt like a representation of the cafe. It was something new that she hadn't mastered. And she'd tried her hardest, but failure still followed on her heels. After years of doing little but working with the Guard, why did she think she could do *this* all of a sudden? It all applied to latte art, and painfully, to running her cafe.

She poured half of her latest attempt into the pitcher and sprinkled cocoa powder over the remaining liquid, to simulate fresh coffee. And then she carefully tipped the pitcher's contents back into the cup, creating a creamy blob. She paused, then added another creamy blob, which flattened the first a little. Then a third blob, all of them nesting together like bowls. So far, so good. And now for the part she always messed up, where she poured a strip down the middle to create a heart-like shape.

She took a deep breath and gave it a shot.

The blobs became blobbier, and not heart-like at all. It broke her.

"Hello! Anyone in here? Almost midnight, you know, that's when everyone wants coffee. In my experience, at least, from fetching coffee on breaks for the other guards. The bastards never want coffee in the day, when everything's open, and then I'm off running around and begging for places to let me in—Gwen? Where are you?"

Jax pushed the kitchen door open to find her sinking down onto the countertop, her face in her hands, her shoulders shaking with sobs. God—of all the things to be upset about, the latte art was what tipped her over the edge? Why was she crying over failed latte art instead of the entire failed cafe?

"Ohhhhh, boy," he said, letting the door close behind him. He took his scarf and coat off, hanging them up with the aprons.

"Crying women isn't my area of expertise, but let's see, I can give it a shot . . ."

Gwen squeezed her eyes shut, continuing to cry pitifully. It hurt. It had all seemed like a dream before she started, yet here she was, having to live with the reality of her choices. She had wanted so badly to try something new that she dove right in without considering how wrong it could go. The price of leaving her comfort zone.

She heard him going through the cabinets, hunting for who-knows-what. Jax always had a weird approach to emotions. After a moment, he muttered, "Aha! This'll do just fine," and then came the sound of the whipped cream bottle.

"Here you go," he said. "Cure for sadness. My mom used to do this all the time when I was a kid."

Gwen opened her eyes to find him holding out a napkin with a cookie on it. He'd sprayed the whipped cream onto the cookie in the form of a smiley face. A laugh bubbled out of her mouth and quickly melted into a sob again.

"Hey, that's pretty good," Jax said, putting the napkin on the counter beside her. "When I was a kid, I'd immediately lick the eyes off. You know, so he'd be blinded? I was a weird kid, let me tell you, my mother had a hell of a time with me. Drove her mad, probably. Well, you've met her, you know how she is."

"You're a weird adult, too," Gwen said, creating a mask for her face with her hands. She peeked at him between some of her fingers, sniffling.

"Yeah, well. They say you can be pretty, funny, or sane, but not all three, and I think we know which one I got." Jax leaned up against the counter next to her, grinning amiably. "Alright, Gwen, spill it. What's going on? Kitchen looks like you had a run-in with a caffeine addict."

Gwen pushed the latte toward him. "It's awful and ugly and a failure," she said. "Just like the cafe." A few tears dribbled free of her eyelids, and she quickly covered her face again. "Don't—don't say anything—I know I sound dramatic, but that's how I'm feeling."

Jax inhaled through his teeth as he looked at the latte, and he nodded slowly. "Well, that's a pretty strong feeling you've got there," he said. "But I don't think it's quite true. You've got that open-mic thing, right? That's going to help you out. Only a few days left, you'll see."

Gwen winced, closing her eyes.

"Whoa, hey, what'd you do to the open-mic night?" he said, straightening. "That was a good idea! Remember that one at the guardhouse, that was something special. Leis got up there and sang *Three Werewolves Meet A Cat.*"

"We're still having it," Gwen said, looking at the countertop. "But I—Mellie and Olympia said we needed so much stuff. I spent the last of what I had saved up to get everything." And she had nothing to say about the Startup Foundation: there was a week until the end of the month. If the event didn't bring up their sales, they were out of time.

"That doesn't mean it won't work," Jax said, thumbing his beard thoughtfully.

"No, but it means if it *doesn't* work, I don't have any savings left to keep the cafe going," Gwen said, glancing at him. "If the Startup Foundation pulls their funding, that's it. There's nothing left. I'll have to . . ."

Jax grabbed her arm. "Don't you say it!" he said. "Don't you get all down in the dumps, 'cause if *you* don't believe in the cafe, then you're guaranteeing your failure. So don't say it."

"I won't say it," Gwen said, wiping her eyes on her sleeve. "But I'm thinking it."

"Don't even think it!"

"I can't stop thinking it! Everything's going to hell, Jax," Gwen said, crossing a set of arms, holding her face in her other hands. "And I don't know what to do about it. I'm doing everything I can, but that's *all* I'm thinking. I can't do latte art, and I can't run a cafe. I *have* to think it, Jax, I can't stop."

Jax sighed. He pushed the cookie toward her. "Come on, then," he said. "Maybe you can't stop thinking about that. And maybe you can't do any more about the event than you've already done. But I'm pretty sure you can eat a cookie."

The cookie didn't turn out to be the cure for sadness, but she ate it anyway.

They'd set up a microphone at the far end of the cafe and cleared a small space around it. Posters that Olympia designed herself were plastered on the tables, the doors, and all around Embervein. Mellie had posted across their social media and gotten other people to give them 'shoutouts,' whatever that meant. Cupcakes, cookies, and danishes were freshly baked, the espresso machines were steaming hot, and the sun dipped low, tinging the sky with orange and pink like cream in coffee.

And there were already more people in the cafe than there had been the entire last week: five. They were only here to watch the performers, rather than participate, but they'd *bought coffee*. All of them. Five sales—and they were drinking it, too!

"Is it weird that I'm kind of nervous?" Mellie asked, pulling her hair back into a ponytail. Her leaves were green and fresh, rustling as she snapped the scrunchie into place. She'd traded her ripped jeans for whole ones, and her band tee had a non-offensive image on it. Most surprisingly, she wore her apron.

"Not at all," Gwen said. "I'm nervous, too."

Mellie rocked from side to side. "I wish Olympia was here already," she said. "I tried lining up the danishes like she does, but I don't know. It's not as good."

"It's just fine, Mellie," Gwen said with a gentle chuckle.

The door jingled and they both looked up, eyes widening: a group of six, chatting and laughing, went straight to the counter. The person in front looked at Gwen. "Hi! We're here for the open mic night?"

Gwen blinked.

"Gwen," Mellie hissed, poking her in the arm.

"Oh! Um," Gwen said, clearing her throat, "Yes! Um, if you could just put your names down on this clipboard, if you want to participate . . ." She panicked, but then found the clipboard tucked into her apron pocket and passed it over.

Mellie smiled widely. "Can we get you all anything to drink?" she asked, in a shockingly friendly and professional voice. Gwen looked at her in amazement and she made a tiny shrug.

"That would be great," the leader said. There was a momentary conversation and flurry of movement as they passed the clipboard around and discussed drinks. While Gwen waited, the door jingled and more people came in, lining up behind them. That made . . . thirteen—no, fourteen people in here? She hoped her eyes weren't bugging out too much.

"Okay, so, we want three chocolate mocha drinks, a straight espresso in a cup, and can you do a latte with chocolate and caramel at the same time, but with no whipped cream on top?" the leader asked. "Oh, and six danishes, please."

"Yes, that's fine, we'll just—" Gwen froze. If she stopped to take their money, then no one was making the drinks, and the other people in the line would get impatient, and . . .

"I'll take their money, you make the drinks," Mellie suggested, as Gwen remembered that she existed.

Gwen nodded and got to work. They'd never had to deal with a situation like this before; usually, one of them handled the order, the money, and the drink, while the others sat around with nothing to do.

As the cafe slowly filled up with more and more people, they found their rhythm with Mellie at the counter calling out the orders and Gwen making them. Six arms, after all, meant she could mix the drinks faster. And Mellie was doing great with the customers, all smiles and 'enjoy your drink!'

The sky outside darkened, turning the cafe into a warm, bright sanctuary from the cold. All kinds of monsterfolk sat at the tables, their coats draped over the backs of chairs, sipping from their steaming cups. When it got crowded, some people elected to sit outside or stand on the sidewalk together, warming their hands on their drinks. Gwen—when she wasn't preparing drinks—stared at them all in sheer amazement.

She peeked out of the kitchen door as she waited for the espresso machine to heat up. A naga dressed in neat, professional clothes took a seat near the counter, setting his camera in his lap. That would be the writer from the *Embervein Daily*. How Olympia had managed to convince him to come *here* was well beyond Gwen, but she couldn't wait for the interview—once things had quieted down, that was. The espresso machine beeped to let her know it was ready for coffee grounds.

She poured the last of the coffee grounds out. The bag was empty. A quick check of the shelves revealed that they were . . . out of coffee? How was that even possible? She heard the door jingle as more customers came in and felt her heart beat faster. No coffee—but for the first time, all these people *wanted* coffee.

"Gwen, we need another salted caramel," Mellie called as she leaned in, hanging on the door. She seemed to realize her mistake and let go of the door, standing properly. "And they want to know if you can add extra caramel."

Gwen turned toward her and showed her the bag. "We're out of coffee," she squeaked. "There's enough for a few more drinks, but then . . ."

"*Fuck*," Mellie said, and then yelped, covering her mouth. "Sorry! Sorry, that just slipped out—"

The kitchen door opened again and in came Olympia, quickly trading her blazer for an apron. "I'm here! That is *such* an amazing turnout, don't you think? There has to be fifty people out there! I hope it's okay that I brought the boys with me, they've got crayons. And I think we need to bring out the spare tables—What's going on?" She looked at their faces.

"We're out of coffee," Gwen said again.

Olympia paused as she fumbled with the apron straps. "We need coffee and tables," she said, clarifying the situation to herself. "We can figure this out. I can run down to Shahid's to get the coffee, and Gwen can get the tables."

"But then who takes orders and gives out drinks?" Mellie said. "*I'll* run down to Shahid's, *you* can get the tables, and Gwen can run the counter."

"But . . ."

The front door jingled, and then jingled again.

"I'm not strong enough for the tables," Mellie said, "and I don't have enough arms to put together drinks fast enough." She glanced between them. "Come on! Let's go!"

The three of them scattered in separate directions, as even more customers came in. Olympia brought out the tables, which were quickly filled, leaving plenty of folks standing. The cafe was full of a friendly, low murmur as people spoke with one another, and the smell of coffee was almost overwhelming. Gwen made as much coffee as she could, sliding drinks along the countertop to their respective buyers—but soon she could make no more, and there was still a line waiting.

"We'll just tell them honestly," Olympia suggested.

Gwen shook her head, staring at the espresso machines. "We can't," she said. "Coffee is our—our *thing*. There's a coffee cup on the sign. Our reputation . . ."

"Gwen, it's time for the open mic to start, you have to do *something*," Olympia said, glancing at the clock on the wall. "If you won't tell them . . . go up and say a few words, distract them. Mellie should be back any moment."

"Say a few words? What words?" Gwen didn't have a speech prepared outside of *'Hi, welcome, have fun,'* and she'd never been great at public speaking, hence why she hadn't gone for the position of Captain in the Guard. Marin could do speeches. She could do conversations, but not speeches.

"You'll think of something, just go," Olympia said, pushing her toward the door. Gwen swallowed and nodded. She'd think of something. She just had to talk long enough for Mellie to return with coffee from Shahid's.

Simple enough—say something, keep the crowd distracted, not make a fool of herself or the cafe. Oh, gracious heavens, all six of her palms were sweaty.

She made her way across the room, feeling incredibly large among the crowd, though they were happy to clear a path for her. As she reached the microphone, she spotted Jax waving from the door, followed by several other guards. This did not help her nerves any. If she embarrassed herself in front of the crowd, the person from the paper, *and* the Guard, she would never, ever be able to forget it.

She leaned down to the microphone. The crowd quieted, and for a moment, the anticipatory silence felt like it would swallow her up.

Gwen cleared her throat.

"Hello, everyone!" she said. Her voice roared from the speakers, startling her. Olympia gave her a reassuring thumbs-up from behind the counter, though she peeked into the kitchen anxiously. "Hi, um—I'm Gwen, and this is my cafe, and I want to say thank you to everyone for coming."

What else? Surely there was something—oh, gratitude always went over well in situations like these. "I also want to take a moment to thank my coworkers Mellie and Olympia," she said, pausing to find the rest of the sentence, ". . . because they planned nearly all of this on their own."

The crowd clapped; she hadn't been expecting that. It almost threw her off, but she plowed ahead. "I should also thank my dearest friend, Jax, for all of his unpaid help," she said, pointing at him in the back. He gave an exaggerated bow as some folks turned to look at him. Jax would have done well with this microphone, much better than Gwen with her fumbling and uncertainty. She looked around for inspiration, and saw some new people sitting at tables.

"He built most of these tables himself," she said. Oh, but that wasn't everything Jax did. "And physical help aside, he always believed in my dream, even when *I* didn't believe in my dream." That covered nearly everything. Oh, no, she had nothing left to say! Who could she thank next? Individual members of the Guard?

Olympia disappeared into the kitchen. Gwen forgot to speak, waiting to see if Mellie was back; a moment later she darted out with two thumbs-up, and Gwen let her shoulders sink with relief. Mellie appeared to take orders.

Time to get things started, for real.

"And we'll be letting everyone use the mic in the order their name is on the list," Gwen said, holding up her clipboard. It took her a moment to read the first line of pinched writing aloud, then she finished with, "Thank you and have fun!" And then she dashed back to the safety of the counter as though chased.

There was a flurry of activity as they served the few remaining customers. Across the room, a vampire with a guitar took a moment to tune before playing a folk song, and soon, the line dispersed, leaving the space behind the counter relatively quiet. Gwen slumped onto the pastry case to catch her breath.

"You spoke wonderfully, Gwen!" Olympia said, grinning widely. "Short and to-the-point. Absolutely perfect. Excuse me for a moment, I should check on the boys." She made her way through the crowd. The little minotaurs had scattered their paper and crayons across a table and were hard at work on a new masterpiece.

"I only heard the last part, but I thought you did great," Mellie said. She wiped her face with a napkin and sat down on her stool, tapping her shoe on the floor.

Gwen blushed. "I was nervous," she said, shaking her arms to get the extra energy out of them.

"You didn't look very nervous," Mellie replied with a shrug.

"A rousing speech!" Jax called from the other side of the counter, clapping his hands together twice. "Look at this place, Gwen, it's amazing—are you even allowed to have this many people in here? You got the papers for that?" He was joking, but then he saw her panicked expression. "No, I'm sure it's fine! It's fine, don't worry about it."

"Um," a tiny voice said. "Excuse me. Um, excuse me . . ."

Gwen looked over the counter to find the two little minotaurs presenting a piece of paper to her. Behind them, Olympia beamed like a lighthouse. "Don't be shy," she said. "You can show her."

Elias rocked on his hooves, looking around. "We drawn it," he said.

"*Drew* it," his brother said, chewing on his hoodie string. "You gotta say *drew* not *drawn*."

"We *drew* it. For you."

"For the fridge," Valisus said, holding it up to Gwen.

Gwen leaned down and took the paper from them. It showed three stick figures, one green with carefully-drawn peg legs, one brown with horns, and one black with eight—Well, it was more than eight legs, but the idea was there. And two little horned boys were floating in the sky above them, next to the sun.

The boys were labeled *ELI* and *VAS*. The green one was labeled *MELLY*, as expected; the brown one was labeled *MOMMA*, also unsurprisingly. And the many-legged one was labeled *NANA*.

Gwen's eyes filled up with tears.

Jax peeked at the paper and laughed. "Oh, you've gone and done it now, boys," he said, ruffling the fur on their heads. "Nana Gwen's going to spoil the two of you *rotten*, just mark my words."

The door to the cafe burst open with a loud jingle, earning startled glances from various people enjoying breakfast. Only four days had passed since the open-mic night, but word had gotten out and the cafe had been busy from open to close. Jax dashed up to the counter with the other guards trailing behind him. "The interview!" he shouted, waving a newspaper.

Gwen glanced up from the cups she was replacing. Her eyes widened. "Is it— have you read it already? Did they say good things?"

"They said *great* things," Jax said, grinning.

"He's right, they said wonderful things," Marin said from behind him. The other guards nodded in agreement as Gwen took the newspaper.

"Mellie!" Gwen called over her shoulder. "Olympia! Our interview is in the paper!"

Mellie stumbled as she ran out of the kitchen, grabbing onto Gwen's arm for support; Olympia followed on her heels, apron covered in flour and frosting. Gwen proudly presented the paper to them.

"What does it say?" Mellie asked.

"Good things, I hope?" Olympia said.

"She hasn't read it yet," Jax said, laughing. "Come on, Gwen, you have to read it first, on account of it being your cafe and all."

Suddenly nervous, Gwen looked down at the paper. On the front was a picture of everyone—Gwen, Olympia, Mellie, Jax and the two boys, as well—smiling in front of the cafe. Her eyes skimmed over the article, jumping sentences to get to the best part, and then she read it again, more thoroughly.

"'The best coffee in Embervein'?" she echoed, passing the newspaper to Mellie and Olympia, who scooted together so they could both read. "That feels—oh, it's very nice, but surely, it's an exaggeration." She laughed.

Jax shrugged. "I think your coffee's good," he said. "But . . . the best? I don't know about—"

Marin kicked his foot.

"Okay, okay, I think it's the best," Jax said, laughing. "You know, Gwen—the paper says you're learning to do that nice art with the lattes, right? Some of the lads were wondering if you could make a little something to show off." He put his hands behind his back and looked upward with all the innocence of a dog holding a shoe.

Marin cleared his throat. "And possibly take pictures of," he said, meeting Gwen's eyes rather stoically given the situation.

"To put on our social media pages." Behind him, Roberta squeaked and clapped her hands. Jax smiled hopefully.

"Well, I could give it a try," Gwen said, squaring her shoulders for the challenge ahead of her. "A try can't hurt anything—but I make no promises."

The cafe quieted as she collected her supplies. She brewed some fresh espresso and put it in a clean paper cup, and then she steamed the milk, double-checking the consistency—not too thin, not too thick. Finally, she laid these things out on the counter in front of her former coworkers, and took a deep breath.

She poured some milk in circles around the cup, letting it swirl and mix with the espresso to get a creamier color. Then she lifted the cup and poured in the remaining milk—frothy, bubbly, creamy—moving the pitcher from side to side. The milk formed a pattern on the surface of the coffee; as she continued, the pattern began to look more and more like leaves. Finally, she put in a singular blob, lifted the pitcher and poured a stream of milk all the way across.

In the cup rested a heart-shaped flower, encompassed by leaves of ascending sizes.

It was *far* from perfect—the leaves on the left side were bigger than the leaves on the right—but it was recognizable, at least. She presented the drink and looked up at their faces, anxiously awaiting a reaction.

"Damn!" Jax said. "That's a flower, alright."

Olympia gasped. "Gwen, that's lovely!" she said.

Marin cleared his throat, examining the cup with a critical eye. He was a Captain, even off-duty: a little stiff, very calm, his emotions kept tight to his chest. And he'd never been one to withhold an honest opinion to spare someone's feelings. If it wasn't what he expected, he'd let her know.

His eyes traced over the colors of pure white and light brown, the shapes of the leaves, the stem, and the heart-shaped flower on top. And then, dutifully, he pulled out his phone and took a picture. Gwen laughed in delight.

"I'm very fond of flowers," Marin said, as gruffly as he could manage while tearing up. "Gwen—I hope you know how proud we are of you. This cafe, and your . . . latte art, are shining symbols of your success."

"Captain . . ." Gwen dabbed at the corners of her eyes and offered him a napkin. "Don't go all sappy on us . . ."

"How much?" a cold voice asked.

Startled, Gwen looked up. Dressed in a plain grey suit, briefcase in hand, was Mr. Manifest; perched on his shoulder was Mr. Eve. They carefully made their way through the cluster of guards.

"I—I'm sorry?" Gwen asked.

"My partner would like to purchase a drink," Mr. Manifest said, barely blinking. He put a small envelope on the counter. "We're here to drop off next month's check from the Foundation. Your new numbers are quite satisfactory. And, to celebrate, my partner would like to purchase the best coffee in Embervein, preferably with a flower displayed on it."

The owl, Mr. Eve, cooed in agreement.

"So again, I ask," Mr. Manifest said, "how much?"

"Free," Gwen said quickly. She pushed the coffee cup toward them with an uncertain smile. "On the house, for friends. Thank you so much."

Mr. Manifest picked up the coffee cup. "It's hardly good business to give out . . ."

The owl nipped his ear. ". . . However, my partner and I thank you for the coffee, and congratulate you on your success." He paused. "Congratulations, Gwen Khetosni."

They left, the owl's eyes fixed on Gwen the entire way. Once outside, the owl fluttered off Mr. Manifest's shoulder. The air warped, and the owl became a bald man in a tweed suit and an eyepatch; he kissed Mr. Manifest on the cheek and took the coffee, his eyes creased with excitement. He waved to Gwen and followed his partner to their car.

"Hey, Gwen," Jax said, "you remember when you were all heartbroken and thinkin' you weren't going to make it?"

Gwen nodded, hiding her face with her hands.

Jax grinned. "Well, look at that, you *did* make it," he said. "If that ain't an 'I made it', I don't know what is. Funny-looking guy, though, reminds me of that time we visited the sauna outside of—have I told this story before? Stop me if it sounds familiar. But this sauna . . ."

Gwen let him tell the story, ushering him and the others to the side so she could take orders from people coming in. The regular sounds of the cafe had turned from silence into pleasant, gentle chatter. It was a far cry from the building she'd bought: empty, falling apart, probably a safety hazard. Now it was warm and full of life, and . . . more or less, everything she'd hoped and believed it could become.

So trying something new hadn't turned out too badly, after all.

Author's Note

If you enjoyed this story, it would mean ever so much to me if you would leave a review on your favorite platform. I am a queer and disabled author and I can only do but so much to promote my work; reviews go a long, long way toward helping others discover my works.

Furthermore, you might consider visiting my website—www.cozyote.com—and signing up for my old-fashioned mailing list so that I can email you fanciful tales of a writer's life (and let you know when my next book comes out).

Thank you very much. I'll get on with the author's note now.

This was the first book I ever published and I hold a certain affection for it in my heart. I'm inclined to feel that my later books are better—but this book holds the very first sparks of my love for cozy fantasy, and I think it shows in the writing. It's been a delight getting to work with it all over again to create a print version.

This book was also my first taste of success! Long after I released *Coffee, Milk & Spider Silk*, I was starting to feel a bit down. I think every writer goes through this—feels that their work isn't worth much, senses their creativity draining away in the face of discouragement. I had the sense that I was only writing for myself—which is no small thing! But seeing as I've always dreamed of connecting with others, it did make me sad. I was very hard on myself. I told myself it would never get better than this.

Around this time, a small cozy fantasy community discovered this story and shared it with each other. And let me tell you, it is an absolutely wild feeling seeing the title of your own book while scrolling the internet! I swear my eyes bugged out.

Many people said wonderfully kind things about my story, and some even emailed me or tagged me online saying how much they loved it. I owe a lot to their words of encouragement. They didn't need to be so generous, but they were, and it renewed my motivation. I wanted—*want*—to create more stories they would love. This passion continues to carry me forward daily; when I feel down about my writing, I remember that there's people out there who found joy in my creation, and I feel inspired to go on.

I saw many requests from them for a paperback version—eBooks are lovely and all, but they can be quite hard on the eyes—and so I immediately began planning out how to do that. I taught myself to typeset (if you're reading this, I hope I did okay!), had some art made for the first page and got to work. It's been a fantastic adventure. I love learning new skills, no more than when I can use them for others.

So for the community that was kind to me when I struggled to be kind to myself, I offer you this: a physical version of the story you love, and . . . one more thing.

You see, many people have asked if there might be a sequel. Lollipop Monster Shop is the second story in the Embervein Emporia, but it's not a true continuation of Gwen's story. (Though, if you haven't read it yet, I encourage you to—I think you'll like it quite a lot.) And while Gwen is gentle by nature, there's another side to her, the protective side of her, the part of her that spent thirty years in the Ember Guard, that I've been dying to explore . . .

For my cozy fantasy community, and for you, dear reader: a brand-new scene that comes after the events of *Coffee, Milk & Spider Silk;* a taste of what's to come.

I hope you enjoy.

Warmly,
Coyote JM Edwards

Seven Years Later . . .

There was a customer waiting at the counter as Gwen came out of the kitchen, and they began placing their order well before she could ask them what they'd like to drink.

"A strawberry vanilla with rainbow sprinkles, please, and if you could just use the Dark Night roast and not the Silly Bunnies roast? Olympia told me you ordered more Silly Bunnies roast even *after* we told you it has, like, the opposite of rizz."

Gwen laughed with delight and dashed forward. "Mellie! Or—should I say, Greenhorn-Private Mellowmalt," she corrected herself with mock-solemnity, unable to keep her smile from pushing through.

"I mean, just Mellie is fine." Mellie glanced down and smiled bashfully.

She looked so grown-up in her maroon uniform, with her name emblazoned across her chest and the familiar tools hung from her belt: a radio, an emergency spell ward, a flashlight, and her plush lemon-cat.

This last one had not been part of Gwen's toolset—it was a celebratory gift from Olympia's boys—but she was delighted to see that the latest recruits were still encouraged to carry personal items for good luck.

Of course, new clothes did not change Mellie's fundamental self-expression: her eyeliner was so dark and smudged she might have been a panda, and little tattoos decorated her arms. Her soft green skin was dark with a healthy tan, and the vining leaves of her hair, kept short these days, were lush and flourishing, and that's what Gwen cared about most.

Gwen beamed. "One strawberry vanilla with rainbow sprinkles, coming right up," she said. "You're lucky—we're almost out of Dark Night."

Mellie rolled her eyes. "Get rid of Silly Bunnies," she called as Gwen went to the kitchen. "Dark Night is obviously superior!"

It was a quiet day in the cafe. Rain came down in sheets and splashes on the sidewalks outside, turning the city into a watery haze. A few moth-people sipped berry mochas in the corner, but otherwise, the cafe was empty and warm. Gwen had made a safe haven from the world outside.

And yet, part of her ached a little, seeing pedestrians running with umbrellas and anti-rain spells; in keeping the world out, she felt a little like she'd trapped herself *in.*

She made Mellie's drink and brought it to her at one of the taller tables. Mellie took it gratefully. "Are these the new *reusable* mugs?"

"They are," Gwen said, and added, "I still think it's unnecessary to call them reusable—*all* mugs are reusable, but—"

"But the advertising," Mellie said with a smile.

Gwen nodded, unable to stop herself from smiling back. "I listen to my experts," she said. "The program is doing well so far. Nearly every other customer chooses a mug over a plastic cup." The whole thing was Olympia's idea. She had a plan to phase out single-use cups by next year, which seemed very ambitious to Gwen. People really seemed to like the mugs, however, and she was all for helping the environment.

She took a drink of her own oat milk latte. "How are you liking your patrol route?" she asked.

Mellie's eyes lit up. "It's so cool! I'm taking the evening-to-late shift right now."

"Oh, the sunsets..." Gwen said. Walking around Embervein at sunset was truly something special. It warmed her heart to think that Mellie would get to experience that, too, now; at the same time, though, she felt a twinge of sadness for what she'd lost. She couldn't really see the sunset from her place behind the counter; the colors dusting the buildings, yes, but not the sky.

"They're awesome," Mellie said with a grin. "I'm still getting to know everyone on my route, but I really love it. I'm glad I took Downtown. Training in Upper Istamour was, y'know, *fine*, but I actually know the area here."

"Knowing the area is important," Gwen agreed, nodding. "None of the other guards are giving you a hard time, are they? I'm happy to have a stern word with anyone," she added.

"I did accidentally drop my radio down a sewer grate on my first night. They're not letting me forget that one in a hurry." Mellie laughed, rubbing the back of her neck. "But no, everyone's been really kind and supportive. And you know Cousin Jax is always around."

"He's not letting them tease you too much, is he?"

"He's joining in!" Mellie said, and they laughed together. She took another drink from her mug and looked down at the dissolving sprinkles, hesitating. Finally, she said, "Y'know, you spend a lot of time indoors, right? Just, like, taking care of the cafe."

Gwen nodded. Where was this going?

"You get this look on your face whenever me and Jax talk about work, like you miss it a lot," Mellie said. "Don't you want to get out more? Y'know, like, leave the cafe? When's the last time you actually went somewhere?" She glanced up briefly, but looked back down at the table, tracing a groove with her fingernail. There was something more to this, something she wasn't mentioning. Despite her curiosity, Gwen decided to let her say it in her own time.

"I like the cafe," Gwen said with a gentle laugh. "I do miss working in the Guard, but I love it *here*." That wasn't quite true though, was it? All the time she spent looking out the window, envious even of people walking in the rain . . .

Mellie took a deep breath and laid her hands flat on the table. "So," she said. "You know how the Guard does a big party when the trainees get their badges?"

Gwen nodded. She recalled hers well—Jax had gotten a lemonade pitcher stuck on his head. This seemed to be a completely different topic from Gwen's increasing wanderlust, but she remained patient.

"I had a few drinks," Mellie said, in a too-casual voice. Goodness, the idea of Mellie drinking—she was technically an adult now, but Gwen couldn't help the feeling that she was still too young. "I did get, y'know, maybe too drunk for the occasion. And I—well, I don't *remember* doing this, but—I, um," she cringed, "I bought a ... food cart? Like, an entire, giant food cart. I have no idea what to do with it. I asked Jax if I could park it at his house and he said absolutely not—and I thought, well, it's rigged for a centaur to pull ..." She gave Gwen a hopeful look. "Do you want it?"

A food cart! The possibilities blazed in Gwen's mind like stars. She could be out and about in the city and bring her cafe with her. Not sheltered from the world, but a breathing, moving part of it. She imagined carefully pouring thick cream into a mug with a cool breeze rustling through her hair, the sound of cars and people passing by, the scent of coffee mixing with the mint-and-petrichor smell of downtown Embervein. It would even give people more opportunities to return their "reusable" mugs, which Olympia had been fretting about.

Could she possibly pass this up? Surely there were downsides to consider . . .

"It's okay if you don't," Mellie said quickly. "Just, like, don't tell my moms?"

"I'll take it," Gwen said, without even trying to consider a single downside. She knew in her heart this was right. And besides, the last time she tried something new, it had worked out *beautifully*.

Acknowledgments

Thank you very much to Brooke and Honor for beta-reading! The story wouldn't be half as good without their help.

As well, a special thanks to my Gramma for proofreading! She has a keen eye (and a lot of patience).

Thank you to my dear friend Raps, known as *supernatural_raptor* on Instagram, for coming up with the title for this story!

I have my most beloved Elk to thank for the spiderweb coffee illustration on the first page. That someone believes in my work enough to make art for it delights and inspires me inexpressably.

Lastly, I am grateful to my wonderful mother for her work on the official description for this book. If it convinced you to read *Coffee, Milk & Spider Silk*, then you and I have her to thank.

Credit for the beautiful cover art goes to Chamika Dilshan, known as *primegpx* on Fiverr.

photo by Elk Johnston

COYOTE JM EDWARDS is a lifelong storyteller and aspiring author. Fascinated by emotion, Coyote seeks to bring a sense of depth and honesty to her work as she explores the stories of non-human people. Her books tackle her favorite topics such as found family, committed platonic relationships, and what it means to trust in others. She walks with a cane, enjoys copious amounts of sushi, and spends her nights preparing tabletop games for her friends. When she writes, it's in bed with a tabby cat on one side and a Labrador on the other.

www.ingramcontent.com/pod-product-compliance
Lightning Source LLC
Chambersburg PA
CBHW010935120626
46552CB00010B/3261